W9-ATY-698

THE VIETNAM WAR

BY TOM STREISSGUTH

The Child's World®

Published by The Child's World®
1980 Lookout Drive • Mankato, MN 56003-1705
800-599-READ • www.childsworld.com

ACKNOWLEDGMENTS
The Child's World®: Mary Berendes, Publishing Director
Red Line Editorial: Editorial direction
The Design Lab: Design
Amnet: Production
Content Consultant: Kenneth J. Heineman,
Professor of History, Angelo State University

Photographs ©: AP Images, cover, 11, 15, 20, 21, 28;
The Design Lab, 5; PH2 Phil Eggman, 6, 26; Department
of the Air Force, 9; PFC G. Durbin/U.S. Marine Corps, 12;
White House, 17; Nick Ut/AP Images, 19; U.S. Air Force, 22;
White House/AP Images, 25

Design Elements: Shutterstock Images

ISBN 9781631437113
LCCN 2014945404

Printed in the United States of America
Mankato, MN
November, 2014
PA02243

ABOUT THE AUTHOR

Tom Streissguth was born in Washington, D.C., and grew up in Minnesota. He has worked as a teacher, book editor, and freelance author and has written more than 100 nonfiction books for young readers. In 2014, he founded The Archive, a publishing company that compiles the nonfiction works and journalism of renowned American authors.

TABLE OF CONTENTS

CHAPTER ONE

THE BATTLE FOR HUE

★ ★ ★

U.S. Captain Jack Chase watched his soldiers run into position. Dozens of them crouched low and fired their weapons. The United States and South Vietnam were working together in 1968. They wanted to stop North Vietnam's **Communist** government from taking over the whole country of South Vietnam.

South Vietnamese and U.S. soldiers' target was a cemetery where the enemy was hiding. Captain Chase's soldiers rushed the cemetery gates. The North Vietnamese soldiers had made the Hue cemetery in South Vietnam into a fortress. The battle of Hue had begun.

THE TET OFFENSIVE

Days before, the North Vietnamese army surrounded the city of Hue. The soldiers knew people were not expecting an

UNITED STATES

VIETNAM

N
NW   NE
W   E
SW   SE
S

U.S. Marines fight back against enemy soldiers in Hue, South Vietnam.

NAVY SEALS

The United States sent Special Forces teams to fight in Vietnam. Platoons of Navy SEALs fought along rivers. The SEALs attacked enemy positions and took prisoners. While on a mission, they wore dark camouflage clothing and face paint. The **Viet Cong**, North Vietnamese allies living in South Vietnam, grew to fear the SEALs. They knew the SEALs as the "men with green faces."

attack. They were preparing for new year celebrations. The North Vietnamese soldiers hid behind walls, fences, and trees. They fired on civilians and U.S. soldiers. The U.S. soldiers fired back.

The North Vietnamese soldiers sought protection in Dong Ba Tower. Delta Company of the U.S. Marines quickly moved to attack the **citadel**. The deadly gunfire continued for hours. Finally, Delta Company captured Dong Ba Tower.

A HARD VICTORY

Finally, the North Vietnamese soldiers retreated from Hue. The Tet Offensive was over. U.S. and South Vietnamese troops took control of the city. But North Vietnam proved it could attack a major city. No one in South Vietnam was safe.

The fighting took Americans back home by surprise. Shocking scenes of war and death appeared on television. Many people demanded the U.S. government bring the troops home. But it would be five years before U.S. troops left South Vietnam.

ANOTHER VIEW

The Vietnam War was the first war to be covered on television. Scenes of battle appeared on the news each night. The news programs also counted the number of soldiers killed and injured each day. What do you think it was like to be an unarmed reporter in a war zone? Why would someone risk his or her life so that people at home could see images of the war?

CHAPTER TWO

THE VIETNAM WAR BEGINS

★ ★ ★

Vietnam is a nation in Southeast Asia. In the late 1800s, Vietnam became a French colony. French settlers moved to Vietnam. Vietnam eventually rejected French control in the 1950s. Vietnam was divided between North and South. A Communist party government ruled North Vietnam. The leaders of North Vietnam wanted to unite the north and south regions of Vietnam. South Vietnam did not like communism. The U.S. government feared the spread of communism to South Vietnam and elsewhere. The United States and South Vietnam became allies.

Many people in South Vietnam opposed President Ngo Dinh Diem.

THE COUP OF 1963

In 1963, Ngo Dinh Diem was president of South Vietnam. He broke many laws. Diem also imprisoned and killed hundreds of Buddhists. Protests against Diem often broke out in the capital of Saigon. On November 1, 1963, a **coup** took over the government. Soldiers guarding Diem killed him on November 2.

Diem's death led to more unrest in South Vietnam. The United States sent military advisers to help fight Viet Cong soldiers attacking South Vietnamese army bases. The Viet Cong were North Vietnamese allies living in South Vietnam. They often struck at night or in the early morning. U.S. Navy ships sailed off the coast of Vietnam. They watched for enemy soldiers. Bombers and helicopters buzzed over the countryside, searching for the Viet Cong. The U.S. air attacks destroyed villages and killed many civilians.

HO CHI MINH

Ho Chi Minh became president of North Vietnam in 1945. When he was young, he had traveled many places. He began to accept the Communist system of government. As leader of North Vietnam, he wanted to reunite the country of Vietnam. He promised independence for all. Ho died in 1969. The war with the United States continued. Eventually Vietnamese leaders renamed the city of Saigon to Ho Chi Minh City.

GULF OF TONKIN

In early August 1964, North Vietnamese boats attacked U.S. Navy ships stationed in the Gulf of Tonkin. The attacks worried President Lyndon Johnson. He asked the U.S. Congress to discuss the Gulf of Tonkin Resolution. It was passed on August 7. This allowed President Johnson to send more troops to South Vietnam.

Soon after, more U.S. Army and U.S. Marine Corps troops

U.S. Secretary of Defense Robert McNamara points out on a map where U.S. Navy ships were attacked in the Gulf of Tonkin.

arrived in South Vietnam. Some troops remained in Saigon and other cities. Others moved to bases in the countryside. These soldiers patrolled jungle tracks and country roads. They searched homes and villages for Viet Cong soldiers. The United States used spies to search for Viet Cong soldiers disguised as civilians. Some Viet Cong soldiers were taken prisoner.

Some Viet Cong soldiers dressed as civilians in order to trick U.S. and South Vietnamese soldiers.

Many **firefights** broke out between the two sides. U.S. soldiers were well trained. They had modern weapons and help from the air. The U.S. troops could call in helicopters and bombers to attack enemy hideouts. The Viet Cong could not fight the U.S. soldiers in the same way. But they, too, had effective methods. The Viet Cong staged quick attacks.

They attacked at night and moved away quickly. They also used hidden bombs and explosive mines.

The Viet Cong and North Vietnam knew the U.S. military was very strong. They knew they could not win big battles. Instead, they planned to wear down and outlast the U.S. soldiers. They wanted to make the war unpopular in the United States. Many Americans did not want American soldiers fighting overseas.

ANOTHER VIEW

The Viet Cong was a small army. They were fighting the United States, one of the largest armies in the world. How would you feel if you knew you had to fight one of the most powerful armies in the world? What would make you take such a risk?

CHAPTER THREE

THE TET OFFENSIVE

★ ★ ★

Vietnam was a tough place to fight a war. Many U.S. soldiers lived in small **compounds** in the countryside. They cleared the nearby jungle so the enemy would have a hard time hiding.

U.S. soldiers often had no fresh clothing. They were often sweaty, dirty, and uncomfortable. Bad food and dirty conditions made many soldiers sick.

U.S. troops faced other dangers on patrol. Helicopters dropped them miles from their camps. They walked through the jungle in a single file line. They searched for hidden enemy soldiers. Attacks came without warning.

A U.S. soldier uses his radio to communicate with a helicopter overhead.

The U.S. soldiers used portable radios to call for air strikes. Planes flew overhead to drop bombs on enemy positions. Helicopters raked the jungle with machine gun fire.

A SURPRISE ATTACK

Tet is the new year holiday in Vietnam. The celebration lasts several days. The Viet Cong and North Vietnamese soldiers attacked Saigon during Tet in 1968. They hoped to take control of the capital. This attack took the United

States and South Vietnam by surprise. The troops were not prepared to fight the Viet Cong soldiers in city streets. The Viet Cong roamed Saigon killing hundreds of soldiers from the United States and South Vietnam, along with many civilians.

News of the Tet Offensive reached the United States. TV news programs showed the fighting. This turned many people against the war. They saw the war was not going to be easy or short. Instead, it looked like a long, hard fight.

The Tet Offensive started the spread of the war across all of Vietnam. The fighting destroyed hundreds of small villages, farms, and fields. The Viet Cong lost thousands of soldiers in the bombings and ground combat. They recruited more soldiers. Some South Vietnamese sided with the Viet Cong. Other South Vietnamese were forced to fight against the United States.

In the United States, the war was growing more unpopular. Many political leaders demanded the United States withdraw from

SPIES

The U.S. military recruited North Vietnamese prisoners as spies. The spies returned to North Vietnam and sent back information on enemy forces. Most of the spies were caught or killed in North Vietnam. Many South Vietnamese also became spies. Some were civilians working with the U.S. military. Others were journalists. They sent information to the North or helped the Viet Cong.

Vietnam. President Richard Nixon announced a new policy. The United States would turn the war over to South Vietnam. U.S. advisers would stay to assist and train South Vietnamese troops. The bombing campaign would continue, but U.S. troops would begin to leave the country.

Richard Nixon

ANOTHER VIEW

Some Americans opposed the United States' involvement in Vietnam. College students held demonstrations. Even some veterans from other wars protested the war. Some who supported the Vietnam War called antiwar demonstrators unpatriotic. Do you think you can speak out against a war and still support your country?

THE WAR SPREADS

★ ★ ★

The Vietnam War came to a standstill. U.S. troops and planes could not defeat the Viet Cong in the countryside. The Viet Cong could not win battles in the big cities. The North Vietnamese were not strong enough to invade South Vietnam. And the troops of South Vietnam needed weapons, training, and support from the United States.

North Vietnam continued to supply its allies in the south. The Viet Cong used bases in Laos and Cambodia. These countries bordered South Vietnam. President Richard Nixon decided to expand the war. The U.S. military ordered air strikes on Laos and Cambodia. The goal was to destroy Viet Cong camps. But the U.S. air strikes failed to do so. The bombing caused death and heavy damage in those neutral countries.

VIOLENCE AT HOME

Protests broke out in the United States against the bombing of Cambodia and Laos. Protesters demanded the United States withdraw from Southeast Asia. The United States began meeting in secret with North Vietnam. The two sides worked on a peace agreement. The talks took place in Paris, France. Meanwhile, the fighting in Vietnam continued.

Smoke rises after a U.S. air strike on North Vietnamese troops.

Peace talks began while the war went on in Vietnam.

VIET CONG TUNNELS

The Viet Cong soldiers built a system of tunnels near Saigon. The Cu Chi tunnels ran for miles. The Viet Cong used them to move their weapons and supplies. From the tunnels, they attacked the South Vietnamese and U.S. troops. The tunnels were very narrow and small. Soldiers had to crawl through them on their hands and knees. They were dark, dangerous places. After the war ended, the tunnels were no longer used. Visitors to South Vietnam can still climb through the Cu Chi tunnels.

Finally, the two sides reached an agreement. But the South Vietnamese government opposed it. South Vietnam did not want the United States to pull its troops completely out of the country.

THE NORTH INVADES

Despite the South Vietnamese opposition, the United States continued to withdraw its troops from South Vietnam. North Vietnam saw this as a good opportunity. It ordered an invasion of South Vietnam.

The attack began on March 30, 1972. North Vietnamese troops stormed across the neutral ground between North and South Vietnam. They used tanks and heavy artillery to attack. North Vietnamese armies overran South Vietnamese bases in the countryside. The South Vietnamese soldiers staged a counterattack. The fighting pushed back the North Vietnamese army. Approximately 100,000 troops died on both sides.

South Vietnamese people watch as their homes are destroyed by North Vietnam.

U.S. prisoners of war are ready to return home after being released by the North Vietnamese troops.

BOMBING IN THE NORTH

The United States supported South Vietnam with a heavy bombing campaign in North Vietnam. U.S. warplanes dropped bombs on Hanoi, the capital of North Vietnam. The attacks destroyed factories and military buildings. The United States also bombed Haiphong harbor. North Vietnam used this harbor to import food and other supplies.

As U.S. troops left South Vietnam, they abandoned their camps in the countryside. Most moved to large bases on the coast. This movement allowed the Viet Cong to capture and hold more territory in South Vietnam.

Although many U.S. troops were leaving, hundreds of U.S. prisoners of war were still in Vietnam. The Viet Cong held some prisoners in camps in South Vietnam. There were also some U.S. airmen who were taken captive in North Vietnam.

ANOTHER VIEW

U.S. troops searched for enemy soldiers in the countryside. Some Viet Cong soldiers wore civilian clothes and worked as ordinary farmers. To defeat them, U.S. planes bombed many small villages. U.S. troops also burned down homes and took prisoners. Many villagers escaped to live in refugee camps. Some military leaders saw the bombing and raiding as the best way to fight the enemy. Other leaders wanted to use peaceful means. Do you think it was worth destroying the homes of innocent civilians and bombing whole villages to defeat the Viet Cong? What else could the U.S. troops have done to find Viet Cong who were hiding as civilians?

CHAPTER FIVE

THE END OF THE WAR

★ ★ ★

North Vietnam gained little territory after attacking South Vietnam. U.S. bombing had destroyed North Vietnamese heavy equipment, planes, and tanks.

Peace talks started up again between North Vietnam and the United States. In January 1973, they signed the Paris Peace Accords. Once again, South Vietnam opposed the agreement. But the United States wanted to completely withdraw its troops and end the war.

A **cease-fire** took place after a treaty was signed. Bombing and ground fighting stopped. U.S. troops began to return home. The United States promised to help South Vietnam if fighting started again.

U.S. National Security Advisor Henry Kissinger and North Vietnamese negotiator Le Duc Tho sign a peace agreement in January 1973 prior to the Paris Peace Accords. ▶

Refugees escape South Vietnam as Saigon falls to the North Vietnamese troops.

FIGHTING RESUMES

The Viet Cong and North Vietnam did not hold to the peace agreement. Instead, North Vietnam attacked in the South. The Communist forces captured many large cities in 1975. Finally they approached the capital of Saigon.

The South Vietnamese army could not fight the enemy advance. The attacks happened quickly and the United States was not able to help. The South Vietnamese government could not supply its troops with enough weapons and ammunition. In late 1974, the South Vietnamese army lost a major battle in central Vietnam.

The Viet Cong moved into the streets of Saigon in April 1975. The city fell into chaos. Fearful civilians packed their belongings and fled to the countryside. Americans took refuge in the U.S. embassy and were airlifted out of the city.

THE FALL OF SAIGON

A huge number of North Vietnamese soldiers surrounded Saigon. The fighting continued in the capital. Enemy tanks rumbled into military bases. South Vietnamese soldiers threw off their uniforms and fled. Artillery shells exploded in the streets. Many civilians died in the fighting.

On April 30, 1975, South Vietnam surrendered to North Vietnam. Vietnam was now unified under a Communist government.

The war destroyed cities, farms, and villages throughout Vietnam. More than 50,000 U.S. troops and airmen died. It is estimated that 2 million Vietnamese civilians were killed, along with more than 1 million North Vietnamese and Viet Cong soldiers. The United States failed to stop communism

REFUGEES

Many people fled Vietnam after the war ended. Fearing the new government, refugees climbed into small boats. The boats left shore at night and soon reached the open sea. The boats were crowded. Water leaked into the boats and many of them sank. Storms and heavy waves struck. Pirates attacked the refugees. They had little food or water, and some refugees died of thirst. Some refugees reached Malaysia, Thailand, and Indonesia. They lived in crowded, dirty camps. Some countries allowed them to immigrate. France, the United Kingdom, and the United States allowed thousands of refugees to settle. More than I million people fled Vietnam by boat after the war.

Protests against the Vietnam War happened across the country, including at the White House.

in Southeast Asia. Cambodia and Laos also fell to Communist governments.

The war divided the people of the United States. Americans argued about U.S. policy toward Vietnam. Some believed the United States should never have become involved. Others saw the United States' withdrawal as a shameful mistake. The arguments over the Vietnam War continue today.

ANOTHER VIEW

The war ended in defeat for South Vietnam. The country fell to the Communist government of the north. The fighting caused heavy damage and many deaths. Vietnam remained poor for many years after the war ended. Gradually, Vietnam recovered. The cities repaired the damage. New factories hired people to make goods. Many U.S. companies began buying products from Vietnam. But the Communist government remained in power. A single political party still runs the country. How do you think the United States should deal with Vietnam now?

TIMELINE

November 2, 1963 | A coup in South Vietnam kills President Ngo Dinh Diem.

August 7, 1964 | The Gulf of Tonkin Resolution allows President Johnson to send more U.S. troops to Vietnam.

1967 | The United States and South Vietnam fight the Viet Cong near Saigon.

January 30, 1968 | North Vietnam attacks during Tet, and the Battle of Hue takes place the next day.

February 1969 | The United States begins bombing Cambodia to disrupt supply routes used by North Vietnam.

1971 | The United States continues to withdraw troops from Vietnam.

March 30, 1972 | North Vietnamese troops storm into South Vietnam.

December 18, 1972 | The United States bombs Hanoi, the capital of North Vietnam.

January 27, 1973 | The United States and North Vietnam sign a peace agreement and agree to a truce.

1974 | North Vietnam steps up attacks in South Vietnam. North Vietnamese troops approach the capital of Saigon.

April 30, 1975 | Saigon falls and South Vietnam surrenders to North Vietnam.

GLOSSARY

cease-fire (SEESS-FIRE) A cease-fire is an agreement to stop fighting a war for a period of time so that an agreement can be made to end the war. A cease-fire took place during the Vietnam War.

citadel (SIT-uh-del) A citadel is a fort that protects people from attack. Dong Ba Tower became a citadel for the Viet Cong.

Communist (KOM-yuh-nist) A Communist government owns land, oil, factories, and ships, and its people have no privately owned property. A Communist government ran North Vietnam.

compounds (KOM-pounds) Compounds are fenced-in areas containing groups of buildings. U.S. troops lived in compounds in the Vietnamese countryside.

coup (KOO) A coup is a sudden change of government brought about by force. A coup overtook South Vietnam.

firefights (FIRE-fites) Firefights are battles with short and fast gunfire. Many firefights broke out during the Vietnam War.

refugee (REF-yuh-jee) A refugee is someone forced to leave a country because of a war or other threats. Many people left Vietnam to live in refugee villages.

Viet Cong (VEE-et KONG) Viet Cong were members of the North Vietnamese Communist movement. Viet Cong soldiers lived in South Vietnam.

TO LEARN MORE

BOOKS

Isserman, Maurice, and John Stewart Bowman. *Vietnam War*. New York: Infobase Publishing, 2009.

Thomas, William. *The Home Front in the Vietnam War*. New York: Gareth Stevens, 2005.

WEB SITES

Visit our Web site for links about the Vietnam War: **childsworld.com/links**

Note to Parents, Teachers, and Librarians: We routinely verify our Web links to make sure they are safe and active sites. So encourage your readers to check them out!

INDEX